Usborne
Royal
Fairy Tales
for
Bedtime

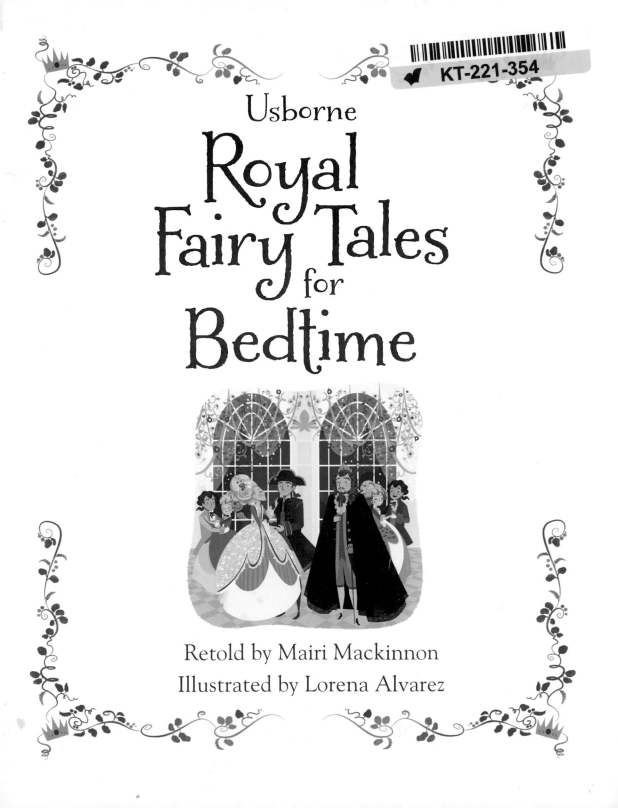

Retold by Mairi Mackinnon

Illustrated by Lorena Alvarez

Contents

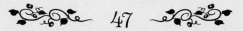

The Princess and the Pea

Once upon a time, there was a prince who wanted to marry a princess. "And she must be a real princess," he insisted.

"Of course she must," agreed his parents, the King and Queen. "We'll send for the royal heralds and announce it at once."

"I think I'd rather find her for myself," said the prince. So he summoned his servants, who packed his bags and saddled the horses, and together they all set out.

The prince went from city to city and from country to country, meeting all kinds of princesses. Some of them were dazzlingly  beautiful. Some were rich and grand, and lived in magnificent palaces. Some were clever, some were gentle and kind. The prince was impressed and he was charmed, but he was never quite sure that any one of them was a *real* princess.

The prince and his servants rode on, further and further from home, to chilly mountain castles and to crumbling desert forts. They found princesses who sang sweetly or danced beautifully, and the prince admired their performances and clapped politely at the end. Some princesses made him laugh, and a few even made him cry. Still, each time he had a nagging doubt: was *this* one a real princess?

"Your Highness, how will you tell?" asked his servants.

The prince sighed. "I can't explain it," he said. "But when I meet one, I'm sure I'll know."

At last, even the prince had to admit that the search was hopeless. Wearily, he made his way home again, and his parents didn't know how to cheer him up.

One evening soon after, there was a terrible storm. Lightning flashed and the rain lashed down, and in the middle of it all there was a knock at the palace door. There stood a girl all drenched and draggled, who said she was a lost princess. A *real* princess.

"With no coach and no servants?" thought the King.

"With no fine gown and jewels?" thought the Queen; but they invited her in all the same, and gave orders for a hot bath and towels and a change of clothes to be laid out for her.

Once she was dry and dressed again, the girl did look a little more like a princess. They all sat down to supper together and the prince thought she was quite charming. The King and Queen smiled to themselves: the prince hadn't looked so happy in weeks.

"My dear, you must stay the night," said the Queen. She ordered a bed to be made up, and went upstairs herself to make sure that everything was done exactly as she wanted.

First, she placed a pea in the middle of the bed. Then she had twenty mattresses piled on top of it, with twenty quilts on top of that. Finally, she had a ladder brought in so that the poor girl could get in and out of bed. It looked a little strange, but nobody said a word.

In the morning, the princess came downstairs looking pale and tired.

"How did you sleep, my dear?" asked the Queen.

"Oh!" said the princess, looking embarrassed. "You've been very kind... but I was so uncomfortable! I could feel a lump somewhere under the mattresses. I've hardly slept at all."

The Queen smiled, and the prince's face lit up. "So sensitive!" he exclaimed. "You *must* be a real princess."

And so they were married, and the pea was placed in a glass case in the Palace museum. Who knows, it may still be there today.

The Frog Prince

There was once a King who gave his only daughter a beautiful golden ball. The princess was delighted with her new toy, and played with it for hours on end.

On hot summer days, she liked going out to the palace gardens, where there were shady trees beside a deep, cool well. One sunny afternoon, she was playing there, tossing her ball high in the air and catching it again. Suddenly it slipped through her fingers, splashed into the murky well water and vanished.

The princess was horrified. "My ball!" she wailed. "Papa's present! How will I ever get it back?" She peered into the well, but the walls were so steep and the water looked so deep, she didn't dare climb in.

"Don't cry," croaked a little voice. "Let me help you."

The princess looked around, but all she could see was a shiny green frog, perched on the well's edge.

"What will you do for me if I find your ball for you?" asked the frog.

"Oh, anything," sobbed the princess. "I'll give you gold, jewels, whatever you want…"

"Gold and jewels are no use to me," said the frog. "Will you be my friend? Will you let me eat with you and drink with you, and sleep on your pillow at night?"

"Yes, yes, I promise, anything," sniffed the princess. "But what's the use? You can't bring my ball back, can you?"

The frog dived into the water, and jumped right out again with the ball clutched between his webbed front feet.

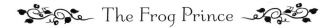

Amazed, the princess snatched it up and ran to the palace. Faintly behind her she could hear a croaking:

"Wait, Princess! I can't keep up with you! Princess! You... pro... mised!"

She ran even faster, not daring to look back. When she reached the door of the palace, she slipped inside and bolted the door behind her.

That evening, the princess was sitting down to supper with the King and Queen when they heard a faint *splash, splosh* outside the hall.

Everyone fell quiet. Then a voice croaked, "Princess! You promised!"

The princess gasped and dropped her soup spoon. She reddened as everyone stared at her.

The King turned to his daughter. "What's this?" he asked. She burst into tears and told her parents everything.

"If you made a promise, then you must keep it," the King said sternly.

The door swung open and the frog hopped into the room. Nobody said a word as he hopped across the floor and then up onto the table beside the princess. She watched in horror as he sipped from her soup bowl. "Delicious!" he said.

The princess made a face and pushed the bowl away. She ran from the table, out of the hall and up to her room, but the frog was right behind her, *splash, splosh, splash, splosh...*

"You're NOT sleeping on my pillow!" the princess shouted. She picked up the frog, screwed her eyes shut and hurled him as hard as she could across the room.

Immediately, she felt ashamed. "Oh, Frog, I shouldn't have done that. I'm so sorry!" she murmured, and opened her eyes.

To her astonishment, there was no sign of the frog. Instead, there stood a kind-looking prince. "Thank you!" he cried. "A wicked witch cast a spell on me. She said it could only be broken if anyone ever felt sorry for me – and who would feel sorry for a slimy old frog? But you've set me free at last."

"Have I really?" gasped the princess.

"So now do you think we can be friends?" he asked.

"Of course!" smiled the princess. "Are you hungry? Shall we go back down to supper?"

The Emperor's New Clothes

Once upon a time, there was a
rich and powerful Emperor.
He ruled over mountains, forests
and lakes, and over towns,
villages and islands.

He wasn't in the least interested in his empire, though, or his palaces and treasures. All he cared about was clothes. He had magnificent outfits for morning, noon and night, every day of the week. He spent hours dressing up to go out, then going out to be admired.

When he inspected his armies, he would ask how *they* thought *he* looked. When he went to the opera or the ballet, he was sure to be more spectacular than anything on the stage. Even so, whenever he put on a new outfit, he was soon tired of it. "It looks so... ordinary," he would complain. "Surely I can do better. I am the Emperor, after all."

One day, two strangers came to the palace gates and made an announcement. "We are weavers of the finest cloth," they said, "and makers of the finest suits. Our cloth is really rather special. You see, only people who are truly intelligent or good at their jobs can see it."

"What a brilliant idea!" thought the Emperor. "With a suit like that, I could soon tell which of my ministers isn't fit to serve me. Only the good ones will be able to see that I'm wearing it. I must order one at once."

The two men were shown into the throne room, where they bowed deeply and murmured, "Your Majesty! We are so flattered! Truly, we don't deserve... Of course, we would be delighted to make a suit for you!"

The men lost no time in setting up their loom at the palace, and asking for bags and bags of gold in payment. They bought reel after reel of bright silks and precious gilt threads, but it was all packed away out of sight. Then they made themselves busy, their shuttles flying to and fro through the empty air.

The Emperor waited impatiently, and after a little while he thought, "I must find out how my suit is coming along." But then a terrible doubt struck him. "What if I can't see the cloth? What if *I* am no good at my job?"

"I'll ask the Prime Minister," he decided. "He's a clever man, he's sure to see it."

So the Prime Minister went to visit the weavers. He was shocked by the empty loom, but he didn't dare admit that he couldn't see any cloth. Instead, he told the Emperor, "Your Majesty, it really is a wonder. So fine! So rich! Such an exquisite pattern!"

At last, the men decided that the cloth should be ready. They took it off the loom, then cut the air with giant scissors. They pinned and they stitched, then proudly brought their work to the Emperor.

"I can't see anything!" thought the Emperor in a panic.

"We can't see anything!" thought all his courtiers; but no one dared to say so out loud.

The Emperor let the men dress him, pulling and patting the invisible cloth. His courtiers pretended to pick up his long cloak, and they all set out to parade through the town.

Everyone had heard about the amazing suit, and crowds lined the streets. They gazed in silence, ashamed to think that they were too stupid to see the wonderful fabric.

Then suddenly a little boy cried: "Daddy! The Emperor isn't wearing any clothes!" Soon the whole crowd was murmuring, "It's true! The Emperor has no clothes!"

There was a sudden gust of wind. The Emperor shivered, but what could he do? He walked bravely on with his head held high.

No one saw the two weavers, shaking with laughter as they scurried away. The crooks crept through the town gate and were never seen again.

The Twelve Dancing Princesses

There was once a King who had twelve beautiful daughters. They slept in twelve beds, all together in one big room at the top of a tower.

Every night the door to their tower was shut, locked and guarded, but every morning the princesses came down to breakfast pale and tired, and their maids found their dancing shoes all worn out.

The princesses wouldn't say where they'd been, and no one else could explain it.

"I won't have secrets in *my* palace," stormed the King. "If you won't tell me, I'll find someone who can. The man who solves the mystery in three nights may marry whichever princess he chooses, and inherit my kingdom after I die."

Soon there were princes and lords lining up to try their luck. The princesses made them all very welcome, and each one was shown to a small room next to the princesses' bedroom. Somehow, though, they never could stay awake through the night...

...and if they failed in their task three nights running, the King had them banished from the land.

One day, a soldier came trudging through the country, home from the wars, and fell into conversation with an old woman on the road.

"That's a strange story about the princesses," he said. "I thought I might try and find the answer myself."

The old woman laughed. "Why not? Just remember, don't drink anything the princesses give you, and pretend to fall fast asleep. Oh, and you may find this useful." She handed him a long, dark cloak. "Wear it, and you can follow the princesses without being seen. Good luck!"

That night, the princesses smiled sweetly at the soldier, and offered him a warm drink. "We made it ourselves," they said. "It's delicious." The soldier thanked them, but he poured it out of a window when they weren't looking. Then he climbed into bed and pretended to snore loudly.

A little while later, he heard the princesses' excited chatter next door. He slipped on his cloak, and tiptoed into their room.

The girls were dressed in shimmering

ballgowns, their faces bright. They had pushed one of the beds aside and opened a trapdoor underneath it. The soldier was just in time to follow them down a winding staircase.

At the bottom of the stairs stood a forest of tall trees, with silver leaves that gleamed in the moonlight. The soldier broke off a silvery twig, and the youngest princess whirled around. "What's that noise? Someone's following us!"

"Don't be frightened, little one," said her sisters. "No one's ever found the way before. That old soldier would sleep through forty fanfares. It's probably just a fox in the bushes."

After the silver forest, they came to a golden one, and then another with leaves of diamonds. Each time, the soldier took another twig and hid it under his cloak. The youngest princess looked around anxiously, but she didn't say anything to her sisters.

They reached a glassy lake, where twelve princes were waiting in lantern-lit boats to row the princesses across. The soldier stepped into the last boat, along with the youngest princess.

"How strange!" said the prince. "I'm rowing as hard as ever, but we're far behind the others. And look how low our boat is in the water!"

On the other side was a castle, with bright lights and music spilling from all the doors and windows. The princes and princesses went in and joined the dancing, and the soldier went with them, skipping invisibly between the couples. Finally, as the sun rose, the princes rowed the sleepy princesses back across the lake.

When they landed, the soldier raced ahead, through the forests and up the stairs. By the time the princesses came in, he was safely in his bed, and they laughed to hear his snores.

For two more nights, the soldier followed the princesses. Sometimes he danced in among them, sometimes he helped himself from the feast laid out between dances: an almond cake here, a handful of grapes there. On the last night, he even slipped a golden goblet under his cloak. Sometimes he snoozed in a corner, but he was always ready to follow the princesses when the princes rowed them back across the lake.

On the third morning, the King summoned him and said, "So, where do my daughters go at night?"

The princesses giggled, then gasped as the soldier produced a velvet bag and took out the precious twigs and the goblet.

"They go through a secret trapdoor to an underground kingdom," he said, "to a castle by a lake. Twelve princes ferry them across the lake to the castle. They dance there all night, and then the princes bring them back at first light."

The King could see from his daughters' shocked faces that the soldier was telling the truth. "You shall have your reward," he said. "Which princess do you choose?"

"Well," said the soldier, "I'm not so young any more. I'd be happy to marry the eldest, if she'll have me."

They were married that same afternoon, and the whole country celebrated their wedding. The dancing went on for a week.

Sleeping Beauty

Once upon a time, there was a King and a Queen who desperately wanted to have children. When at last the Queen had a baby daughter, there were celebrations all through the land.

"We must have a feast for her christening," said the King, and he invited seven fairies to be the baby's godmothers. Each fairy gave the little princess a special gift. "She will be as beautiful as a rose," said the first. "Graceful as a lily," said the second; and the others promised in turn that she would be sweet-natured and talented, she would sing like a nightingale, and dance...

Suddenly, the castle doors burst open and a furious fairy stormed in. She was dressed in a tattered black gown, and her face was creased with spite. Shocked, the guests drew back as she strode through the hall.

"Haven't you forgotten someone?" she sneered.

"Carabos!" whispered the Queen. "We didn't think..."

Glowering over the baby's cradle, the fairy Carabos raised her wand. "*This* is my gift to you," she said. "When you are sixteen years old, you will prick your finger on a spindle and die!"

The guests gasped, and the Queen fainted. Then the seventh fairy stepped forward. "I haven't given my gift yet," she said. "I can't undo this wicked curse, but perhaps I can make it a little better. The princess won't die, but she will fall asleep for a hundred years."

The next day, the King passed a law to ban spinning wool with spindles, and he gave orders for every spindle in the land to be destroyed. Bonfires were built on every town square and village green, and for sixteen years, there wasn't a spindle to be found anywhere.

On her sixteenth birthday, the princess was happily playing hide-and-seek with her friends when she found the door to a distant tower. "I've never seen that before," she thought. Curiously, she climbed the steep stair. At the top was a tiny round room, and an old lady sitting by the window with a handful of wool and a strange, whirling, wooden thing.

"Oh! What are you doing?" asked the princess.

"Spinning, my dear," said the old lady. "Look, I'm making thread. Would you like to try?

But as soon as the princess touched the spindle, she cried out and fell to the ground. The old lady called for help and servants came rushing in, but nobody could wake the princess.

They carried her to her bedroom and laid her down on her bed. As soon as her head touched the pillow, everyone in the castle sank into a deep sleep. The King and Queen nodded off on their thrones, and the lords and ladies slumped on their velvet stools. The cooks in the kitchens, the maids and the footmen, the guards on the battlements, all lay down and slept. Even the horses nodded off in the stables, the dogs drowsed in the yard and the swallows fell silent in the eaves.

A hundred years passed, and a tangle of wild roses grew up around the castle until only the tops of the towers could be seen. The King, the Queen and the princess were all forgotten, and a new king ruled the land.

One day, a prince was riding by, and noticed the turrets above the thorny branches. He couldn't help wondering what lay inside. Jumping down from his horse, he took his sword and started hacking through the wild rose stems.

He reached the castle, and was shocked to see still figures everywhere. "Are they dead?" he wondered; but he quickly realized that they were only sleeping. He wandered from room to room until he came to the princess's bedroom. She was so beautiful that he couldn't resist kissing her.

The princess smiled and opened her eyes.

"Will you marry me?" breathed the prince.

"Oh, *yes*," she said.

The birds started singing and the dogs barked. Hand in hand, the prince and princess hurried downstairs to tell her parents their good news... and slowly the castle came back to life.

The Emperor
and the
Nightingale

Long ago, the Emperor of China
lived in a magnificent palace.
It was surrounded by gardens full of
beautiful flowers, and silver bells
that tinkled in the breeze.

Beyond the gardens was a forest
of tall trees and still, quiet lakes.
Beyond the forest was the sea,
and right next to the sea lived
a nightingale.

The nightingale was a
plain-looking little bird, but she sang
so beautifully that everyone who heard her
stopped to listen and sigh and smile. People
came from far and wide to visit the Emperor's
palace. They wrote long, learned books about
all the wonders they had seen, but they all
agreed that the nightingale's song was the
greatest wonder of all.

In time, the Emperor happened to read
one of these books. He frowned. "What is this
nightingale?" he said. "If it's so special, why
don't I know about it?"

He called for his ministers, but none of them had heard of the nightingale. "Bring it to me!" the Emperor ordered. "By tonight!"

The ministers and the palace servants were all in a panic. If the Emperor didn't get what he wanted, they knew they would be punished, but no one even knew what a nightingale was or where to start looking for one. Finally, a kitchen girl spoke up.

"I know the nightingale. When I go to visit my mother by the seashore, I sometimes hear her singing. It's the sweetest music you ever heard."

"Quickly, show us the way!" said the ministers, and they followed the girl out of the palace.

In the fields, they heard a cow mooing.
"Is that the nightingale?" they asked eagerly.

"No, no," she laughed. "Wait a while."

By the lake, they heard frogs croaking.
"The nightingale, surely!"

"Not yet," she smiled.

They reached the seashore just as the
light was fading. "Hush!" said the girl, and the
nightingale began to sing.

"Beautiful," breathed the ministers. When
the music finished, the grandest of them, the
Lord Chamberlain, cleared his throat. "Little
bird, the Emperor would be pleased to hear your
song. We have come to bring you to the palace."

"My song sounds best here in
the open air," said the nightingale,
"but if the Emperor has asked
for me, I will come."

That evening, the whole court gathered to listen to the nightingale. As she started to sing, the crowds fell still. Silvery notes filled the air, and the Emperor listened with tears in his eyes.

The nightingale's song ended, and the Emperor started clapping loudly. "Bravo! Bravo indeed! Little bird, how can I reward you?"

"There's no need," she said simply. "An Emperor's tears are better than any reward."

From that day, the nightingale was the most important guest in the palace. She had a golden cage, and was allowed to fly out three times a day, with twelve servants holding ribbons tied to her leg. (She didn't enjoy this much, but she was too polite to say so.)

Everyone in the palace and across the whole country talked about the nightingale. Some even tried to imitate her singing, although of course they sounded nothing like her.

One day, a messenger arrived with a gift for the Emperor. "From your friend, the Emperor of Japan," he explained.

Inside the box was a clockwork bird, covered with jewels and with a large golden key. "Another nightingale!" exclaimed the Emperor. He turned the key. "Let's hear them together."

The real nightingale tried to sing along with the golden toy, but she couldn't match its stiff rhythms and mechanical phrases. "The new nightingale is better!" said the courtiers as the Emperor wound it again. "It's prettier! And you know exactly what it is going to sing!" Nobody noticed the real nightingale, quietly flying away.

Soon the toy nightingale was even more popular than the real one. It sang day and night, and its song was easy to learn. Then one day, instead of singing, it made a terrible whirring sound.

The Emperor sent for the royal watchmaker, who opened up the bird and poked and prodded inside. "The mechanism is too fragile," he said. "I will fix it as well as I can, but you won't be able to play it more than once a year."

The Emperor was horribly disappointed. He missed his nightingale badly, and soon became pale and ill. Servants tiptoed through the palace, and ministers began to talk quite openly about who should be the next Emperor. It was as if he had died already.

The Emperor lay in his great carved bed, and in the shadowy corners he seemed to see ghosts, muttering about all the good and bad things he had done in his life. "Hush! I can't bear it!" he cried. He tried to wind up his toy bird, but he was too weak. His eyes filled with tears.

Then a pure silver sound filled the room. The Emperor opened his eyes to see the real nightingale on his windowsill. The ghosts had vanished.

"Dear nightingale," he said. "I've missed you so much. Please come back to stay."

"I can't live in a palace," said the nightingale, "but I can visit you and I always will. My friend Emperor, your ministers are coming. How glad they will be to find you alive and well."

The Firebird

There was once a prince named Ivan who loved riding through the forest with his horse and hounds. One morning, he caught sight of a dazzlingly bright bird through the trees.

Its long wings and tail feathers glowed like fire, bright among the branches. Prince Ivan wheeled his horse around and galloped after it, but however fast he rode, he couldn't catch up.

Further and further he rode. Towards evening he glimpsed the bird again, flying into the gardens of a palace that he had never seen before. Stepping down from his horse, Prince Ivan opened the gate to a magical orchard. All around him were trees bearing golden apples, and eerie stone statues of knights.

Suddenly he saw a halo of light. Tiptoeing

closer, he caught the beautiful bird in his arms.

"Have mercy!" begged the Firebird. "Don't kill me!"

"Kill you?" echoed the prince. "Of course not!"

"Let me go free," she said, "and I will give you this feather. If you should ever need me, I will fly back to help you." Spreading her wings, she soared into the sky.

Left alone, Prince Ivan realized how late it was, and how far he was from home. Just then, he heard the sound of voices. Chattering and laughing, twelve beautiful girls came into the garden, followed by a princess who was lovelier still. They plucked the golden apples from the trees, playing catch with them in the moonlight.

Prince Ivan watched them for a while, then stepped out of the shadows and smiled. "Don't be afraid," he said. "May I join your game?"

By dawn, Ivan had fallen deeply in love with the princess. As the sky grew lighter, though, the girls looked anxious. "We must go back to the palace," the princess said, "and you should leave. It isn't safe for you here."

"Why not?" asked Ivan.

"The palace belongs to the ogre Koshchey," explained the princess. "He is a powerful magician, and we are his prisoners. If he finds you, he will turn you to stone, just like the others."

The prince looked at the statues around the garden and shuddered. "They were once alive?" he whispered. Yet he couldn't bring himself to leave the princess in the ogre's power. He marched up to the palace and wrenched open its great iron doors.

A peal of jangling bells rang out, and a hundred hideous demons spilled into the garden, followed by the ogre himself. Koshchey was furious to see Prince Ivan. He was raising his arms to cast a spell when Ivan remembered the Firebird's feather.

"Help me, please," he murmured.

Light filled the garden as the Firebird swooped down. Fluttering from tree to tree, she led Koshchey and the demons on a crazy dance until they slumped to the ground, exhausted.

"Quickly! Look in the hollow tree," the Firebird called to Ivan, pointing with her long beak. Ivan reached into the hollow and pulled out an iron-bound box. Inside was a gleaming golden egg.

"Take it," whispered the Firebird. "It's Koshchey's soul. Destroy it, and you destroy Koshchey and all his creatures."

The prince cradled the egg in his hands. The ogre jerked awake, screaming when he saw what Ivan had found. Ivan squeezed the egg, and Koshchey doubled up. Ivan tossed it from one hand to the other, and Koshchey flew helplessly through the air.

Finally, Ivan held the egg high and hurled it to the ground. The ogre, the demons and the orchard all vanished in a clap of thunder. All that remained were the statues. As the sun rose, their faces flushed with life and they stretched stiffly, muttering their surprise.

The princess rushed into Ivan's arms, and together they watched the Firebird, soaring away into the heart of the sun.

The Snow Queen

✽❧ Part I ✿✾

Long ago, two children lived in a crowded city, high up in two tall houses that were almost touching. Their names were Kay and Gerda, and they were best friends.

In the summer, they grew red and white roses in their windowboxes, and chatted to each other through the open windows. In the winter, they stayed inside where it was warm, and listened to Gerda's grandmother telling stories.

One December evening, while the snow whirled outside, Grandmother said, "Stay safely here, my dears, and keep away from the Snow Queen. She'll be out there, somewhere, in the thickest part of the storm."

Kay pressed his face to the window, and saw a lady's beautiful white-cold face. She wore

an icy crown, and her eyes glittered like midwinter stars. She waved to Kay and smiled, but he was afraid to look at her and he turned away.

As he turned, he felt a sharp pain in his eye, and another in his heart. The Snow Queen had planted splinters of ice there so that he could no longer see or feel the goodness in anything.

"Grandmother, I don't understand it," said Gerda, a few days later. "Why is Kay so angry and mean? He makes me cry, but he just laughs."

Kay didn't want to play with Gerda any more. "Growing flowers is for girls," he sneered. "Stories are for babies." Instead, he liked going to play with the big boys in the snowy cathedral square.

One afternoon, he saw a splendid silvery sleigh with a driver all wrapped in furs. "Don't you recognize me?" said the Snow Queen. "Come and sit beside me."

Kay thought she was the most beautiful person he had ever seen. She bent to kiss his forehead with icy cold lips. Then they set off, and the snow flurried around them as they swept out of the city gate. Faster and faster, they flew through the air to the Snow Queen's palace.

Kay was gone, and nobody knew what had happened to him. "He often went tobogganing down by the river," said the boys in the square. "Maybe he fell through the ice and drowned." No one except Gerda seemed to care.

In the spring, she went down to the river. "Please bring my friend back," she whispered. "I'll give you my new red shoes." She threw her shoes into the water, but the river just washed them back again. "Maybe I didn't throw them far enough," Gerda thought. Stepping into a boat, she pushed off from the river bank.

The boat began drifting down the river, catching the current and gathering speed, and Gerda couldn't do anything to stop it. "Perhaps at least it will take me to Kay," she thought.

At last, the boat drifted around a bend and on to the bank. There stood a neat little cottage, with an old lady in a sunhat working in the garden. "Can I help you, my dear?" she called. She held the boat steady as Gerda clambered out. "Sit down and rest, you poor thing."

"Such a pretty little girl," thought the old lady. "If only she could stay here forever..." Gently she combed Gerda's hair, soothing her to sleep, combing the memories away. She even cut down the roses outside her house so that Gerda wouldn't see them and remember her home.

The old lady was kind, and Gerda stayed happily enough, although sometimes she found herself thinking that something was missing. Then, one summer morning, she noticed the old lady's sunhat lying on a chair, with its pattern of...

"Roses!" she realized. "Kay!" she cried. "Oh, what am I doing?"

She ran from the house, stumbling through the woods with tears in her eyes, until she had to stop and rest. A curious crow hopped down beside her. "Little girl, why are you crying?"

"Oh, dear crow, I am looking for my friend Kay. Have you seen him?" Gerda told her story, and the crow hopped excitedly. "Maybe I have, maybe I have," he cawed.

"You see," he continued, "our princess recently decided to get married. She advertised in the newspapers, and all the fine gentlemen came calling, but she didn't care for any of them – until a brown-haired boy came along, with shiny black boots that squeaked."

"That's Kay!" said Gerda. "Those were his new boots; he was so proud of them."

The crow continued: "He told the princess he only wanted to talk to her because he'd heard she was so wise. Of course, that impressed her more than anything, so now he is a prince."

"Lucky Kay," sighed Gerda. "Can we go and see him, do you think?"

"I know a way into the palace," said the crow. "I'll show you."

"We'd better wait until night, though," he added. "If they see you, the guards and the footmen will never let you near the prince and princess in those shabby old clothes." He flew ahead of Gerda to the palace grounds, and went to the kitchens to scavenge some bread for her.

That evening, he showed Gerda to a little door at the foot of a tower, and she followed him up the winding stair. At the top was a magnificent bedroom, with two beds shaped like red and white lilies. In the white lily bed, the princess slept soundly.

Gerda turned to the other bed. She thought her heart might burst. Leaning closer, she whispered, "Kay? Is it you, at last?"

The Snow Queen

❧ Part II ❧

The prince opened his eyes.
"Oh!" sobbed Gerda.
"It isn't Kay at all. It looks
just like him, but it isn't."

The prince sat up sharply and the princess woke in a panic, but when they heard Gerda's story, they were truly sorry for her. The next day, they dressed her in velvet and furs and sent her on her way in a gilded coach.

As night fell, the coach came to a dark forest where a band of robbers noticed its golden glow. They sprang out of the trees, seized the horses and dragged Gerda from the coach.

"She looks tasty!" said an old robber woman, brandishing a cruel knife; but a wild girl with curly black hair jumped up. "No!"

she yelled. "I want her to be my friend. She's coming with me in the coach, back to our castle." Gerda was terrified, but she knew the girl meant to be kind.

When they arrived, the girl said, "Come and see my pets." She led Gerda through a high stone hall to a heap of rugs in the corner, where her bed was. Above the bed were a hundred wild pigeons in cages, and next to it was a reindeer tethered to the wall.

"Look at your fancy clothes! Are you a princess?" she asked.

"No," said Gerda, and told her story. "Have you seen him, have you seen Kay?" she asked hopefully.

"We have, we have," cooed the pigeons. "We saw Kay with the Snow Queen in her sleigh, rushing through the air to Lapland. So cold, so cold!"

"To Lapland?" asked Gerda.

"To my country," said the reindeer. "That's where the Snow Queen lives."

77

"Oh, how can I get there?" cried Gerda.

"You must run away," said the robber girl. "I'll help you. Not now, but tomorrow, when all the men are away. You can take my reindeer, but I think I'll keep your clothes, they're much nicer than mine."

In the morning, she gave Gerda some old clothes of her own, and helped her onto the reindeer's back. "Take care of her, now," she told him, flashing her long knife in warning.

The reindeer sped off through the forest, galloping all day across the snowy plains to

Lapland. Just when he was beginning to tire, they saw a distant hut. Gerda tumbled off the reindeer's back, and knocked at the lighted window.

The only person at home was an old woman. "Mercy, however did you get here?" she exclaimed. "Come in and warm yourselves."

When Gerda told her story, the old woman sighed. "Yes, the Snow Queen lives near here, and she has your friend Kay. She's planted ice splinters in his eye and in his heart, too. Oh, he thinks he is happy enough, but he'll never be his old self until he gets rid of those splinters."

"You're very wise," said the reindeer. "Can't you give Gerda some special power to help her?"

"She doesn't need it," the old woman replied. "For a little girl on her own, to have come this far – she is stronger than she knows. Take her to the Snow Queen's palace, and you'll see."

It was only a few miles further to the Snow Queen's palace, but the snow fell thickly and the snowflakes grew bigger, making the shapes of snarling wolves and bears. Terrified, Gerda breathed a prayer – and her breath turned into angel-shapes, marching all around her. The angels beat the snow-creatures away until she could walk freely through the great icy gates.

Inside, she wandered through a hundred snow-filled halls, vast and silent, eerily lit by the Northern Lights. In the biggest hall of all was a great frozen lake, and in the middle of the lake stood the Snow Queen's crystal throne.

The throne was empty: the Snow Queen had gone to whip up blizzards and make mischief in the countries far to the south. Gerda's face fell; and then beside the throne, she saw a figure, white with cold and hardly moving.

"Kay!" cried Gerda. She ran to put her arms around him, and her warm tears went straight to his heart, melting away the ice-splinter there.

Kay looked up, amazed. "Gerda?" he whispered. "You've come all this way to find me?" Tears welled up in his own eyes, washing away the second splinter. The two of them clung to each other, and Kay felt warmth slowly spreading through his body. Then, hand in hand, they walked out of the palace.

The snowstorm had stopped and the sky was clear. On the horizon they could see the bright rising sun, and they followed it southwards.

When they reached the old woman's hut, the snows were starting to melt. In the robber girl's forest there were green buds on the trees, and in the princess's kingdom there were spring flowers in the hedges. Along the river, the apple trees were in blossom, and when they reached the city they saw roses in all the windowboxes.

Gerda's grandmother sat by the open window, dressed in black. When she saw the two children, she could hardly speak for joy. All three held each other close, together again in the warm sun.

The Flying Horse

There was once a king who loved all kinds of magic and mechanical marvels. One day, an inventor presented him with a life-sized ebony horse, patterned with gold.

"Splendid!" said the King. "What can it do?"

"Your Majesty, this horse will fly through the air, faster than the wind," the man declared.

The King's son had been admiring the horse, but now he burst out laughing. "Don't be ridiculous!" he snorted. "How can it possibly fly?"

The inventor glared at him. "See for yourself," he snapped. "Just twist the pin in the right shoulder, and use the reins to steer."

The prince jumped onto the horse's back and twisted the shoulder pin. Everyone gasped as the horse rose high above the palace courtyard.

"How do I get down?" the prince called.

"Ha! You should have thought of that before making fun of me," cackled the inventor.

The prince rose up until he was lost in the clouds. The King raged, the Queen screamed and the inventor was thrown into prison.

Meanwhile, the prince thought: "If there's a pin to make it go up, most likely there's another to come down." Sure enough, he found a pin on the horse's left shoulder, and soon he was swooping down and soaring up through the air.

By evening, he was far from home above a land of green hills and orchards. He saw the domes of a great palace, and came down to land on the roof. Stepping inside, he found a guard dozing by a bedroom door, and in the bedroom was a sleeping princess, so beautiful that he could hardly breathe.

She opened her eyes and smiled shyly. "Who are you?" she asked.

They talked for hours, each finding the other more and more wonderful, until they heard raised voices and the princess's father stormed in. "What thief dares to break into my daughter's bedroom?" he thundered.

"I'm no thief," protested the prince. "I'm a prince who would like to marry your daughter."

"I can't give my daughter to someone who sneaks past my guards," snapped the King. "You deserve to die for your insolence."

The prince thought fast. "Set me a challenge instead," he said. "If I can face your entire army, without a single scratch, then let me marry your daughter."

"Ha!" said the King. "I accept. I have ten thousand soldiers in my army. They'll chop you into ten thousand pieces."

The princess went pale, but the prince smiled to reassure her.

The next morning, the army gathered outside the city gates. It was a terrifying sight, but the prince was calm. "May I at least fight on horseback?" he asked.

"Of course," said the King. "Choose any horse from my stables."

"Thank you," said the prince, "but I'll ride my own horse. You'll find him on the palace roof."

The King's courtiers giggled. When his servants brought the ebony horse, stiff and lifeless, they guffawed. The prince mounted, and the King gave the order to charge.

Slowly, the ebony horse rose into the air. The prince swooped down here and there and the soldiers slashed and stabbed, but he was always out of reach. Then, with a wave, he flew up to the princess's balcony, helped her into the saddle and soared away.

By evening, they had reached the prince's home. As they were landing, the prince saw black pennants flying and heard loud wailing.

"My darling," he said to the princess. "Something terrible must have happened. Wait

for me here in the gardens while I find out what is the matter." He settled the princess and hurried into the palace.

As soon as they saw him, the servants shrieked, "It's a ghost!"

"Ghost?" said the prince. "Was all that wailing for me? I've never felt more alive."

"We thought the old inventor had killed you! He has been thrown into the dungeons!"

"Well then, you must let him go." And the prince went to find his parents, who were overjoyed to see him.

Meanwhile, the inventor wandered into the gardens, raging at his cruel treatment. With delight, he recognized his ebony horse. When he saw the princess, a plan came into his mind.

"My lady," he said, "the prince has sent me to bring you to the King and Queen. Please, mount your horse and we will go to meet them."

"But I don't know how to ride it," the princess protested.

"Then I will show you," said the inventor, climbing into the saddle after her. He twisted the pin and the horse reared up, but he steered it far away from the palace and over the sea. The princess realized she had been tricked, and she cried bitterly, but the inventor only laughed as they came down to land by a distant forest.

The princess shrieked for help, and out of the forest came a king's hunting party, who soon overpowered the inventor. Bringing them back to his palace, the King made fine apartments ready for the princess, and had the ebony horse placed in his treasure chamber.

The inventor was thrown into prison once again, and it's hard to say who wailed louder, he or the grieving girl.

"Your Majesty, she is ill or she is insane," said his courtiers. "No good will come of this."

"Then send for the best doctors," said the King. "I love her, and she must be cured."

Wise men came with potions and tokens, spells and charms, but they made no difference. One day a young doctor came from a faraway kingdom. "I have some experience in that kind of madness," he said. "Let me see what I can do."

When the princess saw him, she fell quiet for the first time since she had arrived. The King was impressed.

"I'm afraid it won't last," said the mysterious doctor. Sure enough, the princess soon began sobbing again. "I can cure her, but we must go back to the place where you met. Bring everything that you found there."

So they went back to the forest with the princess, the ebony horse and the inventor muttering in his chains.

"There is something about that horse," said the doctor. "Let us mount it, and I will cast a spell to stop its evil power. Now, please, stand back."

Suddenly the inventor recognized the doctor. Too late, he screamed in fury as the prince, princess and horse all soared away.

"I am sorry to deceive you, your Majesty," called the prince. "Truly, I hope that you will find the love you deserve."

He took the princess home to his father's kingdom, and their wedding feast lasted for weeks. The ebony horse became one of the King's greatest treasures, but only after he had destroyed its workings. "It will cause less trouble if it never leaves the ground," he said.

Edited by Lesley Sims
Designed by Russell Punter

Additional design by Laura Wood

First published in 2012 by Usborne Publishing Ltd., Usborne House, 83-85 Saffron Hill,
London EC1N 8RT, England. www.usborne.com
Copyright © 2012 Usborne Publishing Ltd.